WE CHOSE YOU

To our ten wonderful children.
God brought us together in an amazing way that only He could orchestrate. We thank you for being the inspiration for this story.

—A Book About ADOPTION, FAMILY, and FOREVER LOVE—

WE CHOSE YOU

NEW YORK TIMES BESTSELLING AUTHORS

TONY & LAUREN DUNGY

HARVEST HOUSE PUBLISHERS
EUGENE, OREGON

"Hey, sweetie! How was school today?" Calvin's mom called as he and his dad walked through the front door.

"Pretty good," said Calvin, hanging up his backpack.

"Calvin has a special assignment for tomorrow," said Dad.

Calvin nodded. "I have to tell the class about my family." He looked worried.

"Can you tell me about our family again? About how you chose me?"

Mom and Dad smiled. “Of course,” said Dad.

Calvin sat down between his parents, and Mom picked up the big red photo album.

"This was the beginning of our family," she said, pointing to the smiling couple cutting a wedding cake.

Calvin giggled at the next picture of his parents with frosting on their faces.

"And it was a great family, but we knew right away someone was missing," said Dad.

Mom nodded. "We spent a long time waiting for a baby. We prayed every day for that baby."

Calvin's eyes grew wide. "*Every* day?"

Dad grinned. "Every single day."

Mom squeezed Calvin's hand. "Waiting for you was the hardest thing we ever had to do, but we believed that God would make us a family someday."

"We searched high and low," his dad said, "and near and far, because we weren't looking for just anyone—"

"You were looking for me!" Calvin exclaimed.

"That's right!" said Dad.

"And when you found me. . . "

"We chose you," Mom and Dad said together.

"You chose me,"
Calvin repeated happily.
Those words always
made him feel special.

“I have an idea,” said Mom. “Why don’t we make a poster about our family for you to use when you talk to your class?”

“Yeah!” Calvin said as he jumped up to get his markers.

A little while later, as Calvin sat coloring his poster, he had another question for his mom.

"If I didn't grow in your tummy, am I really part of your family?"

His mom sat down next to him.

"There are lots of ways to make a family," she said. "Every single family is created by God, but God doesn't create every family the same or in the same way."

Calvin thought about that. “Like how Marcus has four sisters, but Jasmine doesn’t have any?”

Mom nodded. "Or how Kendra lives with her grandma, or Landon lives with his dad and his stepmom. All families are special and important, no matter how they were created."

Calvin looked at his drawing of his family as his mom continued.

"Sometimes God uses a mom and a dad to create a baby, and sometimes He brings them a baby through adoption, like He did with you. He puts together every family exactly the way He wants it."

Calvin looked impressed. “You mean, God chose you and Dad for me?”

“He sure did!” said Mom. “And He chose you for us.”

“Wow,” Calvin exclaimed, “I’m putting that on the poster!”

Mom laughed.

That night as Calvin was getting ready for bed, he had a hard time choosing between his red pajamas and his blue ones. When Mom and Dad came in to say goodnight, they found him looking worried.

“If you chose me, does that
mean you can change your mind?
Like I did about my pajamas?”

“What if you decide you want a kid who is taller or better at math?
What if I get in big trouble? Could you un-choose me someday?”

Dad shook his head. "We didn't choose you because of how you looked, Calvin, or because of your talents or your behavior. We chose *you*, and we love you no matter what you do or what you look like. We would love you even if you had purple hair and green teeth!"

Calvin laughed at the idea of green teeth, and Mom and Dad laughed too, but then Dad's voice turned serious.

“Once we became your parents, we all became a family.
You can’t un-choose family.”

Mom picked up Calvin's red pajamas from the floor. "Nothing about our family was an accident. Psalm 139 says that God had special plans for each one of us before we were even born."

"For you and Dad too?" Calvin asked.

"Oh, yes," said Mom. "Before Dad and I were even born, He knew He was going to make us a family and make you our son."

Dad put a hand on Calvin's shoulder. "When we chose you, we became a family forever."

"Forever," echoed Mom, and she gave him a big kiss. "And now it's time to turn out your light and get some rest before school tomorrow!"

"Yeah." Calvin snuggled down under his blanket. "Tomorrow I'm going to tell my class all about how I have the greatest family ever!"

Cover design by Kyler Dougherty

Interior Design by Left Coast Design

HARVEST KIDS is a trademark of The Hawkins Children's LLC. Harvest House Publishers, Inc., is the exclusive licensee of the trademark HARVEST KIDS.

We Chose You

Published by Harvest House Publishers
Eugene, Oregon 97408
www.harvesthousepublishers.com

ISBN 978-0-7369-7325-0 (hardcover)

Library of Congress Cataloging-in-Publication Data

Names: Dungy, Tony, author. | Dungy, Lauren, author. | Wolek, Guy, illustrator.

Title: We chose you / Tony and Lauren Dungy; illustrations by Guy Wolek.

Description: Eugene, Oregon : Harvest House Publishers, [2019] | Summary: Worried about a school assignment on family because he was adopted, Calvin asks his parents about being chosen and learns that God creates all families, but not always in the same way.

Identifiers: LCCN 2018025866 | ISBN 9780736973250 (hardcover)

Subjects: | CYAC: Adoption--Fiction. | Families--Fiction. | Christian life--Fiction.

Classification: LCC PZ7.D9187 We 2018 | DDC [E]--dc23 LC record available at https://lccn.loc.gov/2018025866

Printed in China

18 19 20 21 22 23 24 25 26 / IM / 10 9 8 7 6 5 4 3 2 1